"What's he *doing here?"*

"I don't mean that he shouldn't be *here* in the United States. I just wish he wasn't here in our gym."

Dimitri's feet were encased in a pair of cheap cowboy boots. They were huge feet. I didn't like the idea of those big feet in *my* gym.

"If he's so famous, how come he wound up in our gym instead of some world-famous gym?" I complained.

"Give Dimitri a chance, Lauren," said Darlene. "I think it will be a thrilling experience for all of us."

I don't like to be *told* that something will be thrilling. It's like a teacher telling you that something is going to be "very interesting." It never is.

**Look for these and other books
in THE GYMNASTS series:**

THE GYMNASTS

#18 THE NEW COACH?

Elizabeth Levy

AN
APPLE
PAPERBACK

SCHOLASTIC INC.
New York Toronto London Auckland Sydney

ISBN 0-590-44695-9

12 11 10 9 8 7 6 5 4 3 2   1 2 3 4 5 6/9

Printed in the U.S.A.   28

First Scholastic printing, July 1991

To George Vickorskoff —
a great coach

THE NEW COACH?

World-class Jerk

My coach, Patrick Harmon, doesn't like us to have grudge matches. But *I* knew that Patrick wanted nothing more than for the Pinecones to beat the pants off our archrivals, the Atomic Amazons. We were scheduled for a series of three meets against the Amazons, and this was the first one.

We were doing our one-touch warm-ups on the vault. This means that you can only touch the horse one time, and then you have to stop your warm-up.

"Okay, Lauren," Patrick whispered to me. "Show them your stuff." I'm one of the best vaulters on my team. I knew the Amazons and their coach, Darrell Miller, were watching, and I wanted to impress them.

However, as I started my run, my rhythm was all off. I stopped on the springboard, being careful not to touch the vault. My hands went forward, but I knew I didn't touch it.

"Okay," said Patrick, "do it again." This time I did a great vault. I landed cleanly. If I could do that in the competition, we'd be sitting pretty. Patrick gave me a high five. I noticed the Amazons' coach whispering to a judge.

Then the judge came up to Patrick. She was dressed in a blue suit. She had gray-blonde hair in an old-fashioned pageboy style. Patrick started waving his hands around. The judge put her hands on her hips. Coach Miller looked smug.

I heard my name mentioned. I went up to them to find out what was going on. "You touched the vault twice," said the judge. "Both Darrell Miller and I saw you. That's a deduction."

"I didn't touch it!" I shrieked. Patrick put his hand on my shoulder. I knew it wasn't good form to shriek at a judge.

"Next time make sure your gymnasts are more careful," said Coach Miller. Patrick glared at him.

Becky Dyson, who is on our advanced team,

was getting ready for her warm-up. "Nice going, Lauren," she said sarcastically. "It takes a real jerk to lose points *before* the meet begins."

"Oh, Becky, hush up," I said. I was really upset. I hadn't done anything wrong. "Patrick, tell the judges that Darrell Miller is a first-class jerk!" I yelled.

"Lauren, lower your voice," warned Patrick. He has thick, curly brown hair and blue eyes. Patrick is young compared with Coach Miller. Normally he's very calm and fair, but I could tell that Darrell Miller had gotten his goat. Patrick had started his professional career as a coach with Darrell Miller, and I knew they didn't really get along.

I bit my lip and glared at Coach Miller. The judge who had ruled against me was staring at me.

Patrick put his arm on my shoulder and guided me over to the corner of the gym where the other Pinecones were looking nervous. I was a little worried that they were going to be mad at me for putting them in a hole even before we began.

Patrick told them what had happened. He said it wasn't my fault, but those were just the breaks.

"Sorry, gang," I said. Jodi and Cindi were looking at the floor. I could tell they were nervous.

Cindi's red hair was sticking out all over the place, the way it does when she can't stop putting her hands through it.

"I said I was sorry," I repeated.

"It wasn't your fault," grumbled Jodi. She looked up and gave me a smile. Jodi twisted her blonde hair into a ponytail. On the outside, Jodi looks like a typical gymnast, blonde and thin. I'm shaped more like Bart Simpson, with muscles for legs. No matter how much I work out, I still look short and squat. "Built like a fireplug," says my dad, as if it were a compliment.

"That one judge really has it in for us," complained Darlene. I think Darlene is drop-dead gorgeous. She's thirteen, two years older than Jodi, Cindi, and me. "Lauren didn't do anything wrong," she said.

I let out a deep breath. Darlene is *not* a complainer, and if she thought I was in the right, I didn't have to worry.

"I think that judge is Coach Miller's first cousin," whispered Ti An. Her hair was pulled back. Ti An tried to look a little older than nine, but she's so tiny that she looks only seven.

"Patrick!" I screeched. "Did you hear Ti An?"

"I told you to keep your voice down, Lauren," Patrick warned me.

"But Ti An used to go to the Atomic Amazons' gym," I argued. "She would know."

Patrick looked over at the judge who had ruled against me. "It so happens that Ti An isn't right. That judge used to be related by marriage to Coach Miller's first cousin, but she's divorced now."

"How do you know all this?" I asked him.

"Gymnastics is a small world," admitted Patrick.

I scrunched up my eyes and turned to look at the judge. She had thin lips. I didn't like her. "I still think she should disqualify herself. Isn't there something in the rule books about it?"

"She's a very fair judge," said Patrick. "It's a proven fact."

Patrick was teasing me. He knows that I say "it's a proven fact" all the time. I interrupted Patrick. "Now what's Coach Miller trying to do?" I objected.

Coach Miller was walking over to the judges' table with a very tall man with a mustache. The judges were standing up and practically saluting this guy.

"Who's that?" I asked Patrick.

"Lauren," said Patrick, sounding a little exasperated, "will you stop looking around and put your mind on what's happening here? We have a meet starting in a few minutes, and I'd like your attention."

"Yeah, but I just know that Coach Miller's got

another trick up his sleeve," I complained.

"He *is* a first-class jerk," said Cindi.

"World-class," I said.

"Becky's only in the pipsqueak-jerk class compared with Coach Miller," said Jodi.

"Girls, you let *me* worry about Coach Miller," said Patrick. "*You* worry about nailing your routines."

"Yeah, Lauren," said Cindi. "We start out with the vault. You can make up that deduction easily."

Patrick agreed. "Lauren, you'll be doing the Yamashita. That should wow them."

I was the only one on our team who could do the Yamashita in competition. It starts out like a regular handspring vault, but when you leave the horse you have to really fly because you throw your legs over your head before you land.

We were hoping that none of the Amazons could do it. At least they hadn't during our last competition.

The judge rang the bell for the competition to begin. We Pinecones all put our hands into the middle of a circle, one on top of the other. That's the Pinecones — we really root for one another.

"Let's go, team!" said Cindi.

"Yeah," said Ashley, "we can still do it, even though we're already half a point behind."

When I said that we really root for one another,

6

I forgot about Ashley. Along with Ti An, she's one of the youngest members of the team, but it was just like Ashley to remind me that I had already put us in a hole.

"It's all that jerk Coach Miller's fault," I said.

"Come on, Lauren," said Cindi. "One good vault and you'll put us ahead! Let's go get 'em."

"Sure," I said. I tried to sound enthusiastic, but I was worried. "I think the judge already hates me," I muttered.

Patrick shook his head. "Lauren, no negative vibes," he warned.

"It's not negative vibes I'm scared of," I said. "It's negative points."

2

Is That a Threat?

"I don't believe it," I muttered.

"Don't believe what?" asked Heidi Ferguson. Heidi had come to the meet late, and she was dressed in street clothes: a pair of black sweatpants and a Bronco sweatshirt. At least she was beginning to wear some brighter colors. Bronco orange was better than all black.

Heidi was standing next to me as we watched the first Atomic Amazon do her vault. I would be the last vaulter, not just for our team but for the whole event.

The other Pinecones had already done their vaults. Ashley did okay, but she did such a simple vault that she scored only a 7.7. Jodi had completely fouled up. Ti An fell on her landing, and Darlene opted to do an easier vault than she had planned, because she told Patrick she just didn't feel ready. Cindi tried a harder vault, but she fell on her landing, too.

It was *not* a great beginning. Then the bottom caved in. The Atomic Amazon in front of me did the Yamashita and stuck the landing.

"Did you see that?" I exclaimed. "That girl just did *my* vault. Patrick said I was going to wow them with that."

Heidi shrugged. I knew my vault wasn't very impressive to her. Heidi wasn't competing at this meet, which was not for elites.

Heidi isn't just an elite gymnast, she is world-class. Heidi, however, is not a world-class jerk, like the coach of the Atomic Amazons.

She's kind of terrific. She had come to our meet just to cheer us on. She's fourteen years old, only a year older than Darlene, but she's light-years ahead of the rest of us in what she can do.

The next Atomic Amazon was up. "If she does it, too, I'm going to bust a gut," I said.

"What's Lauren complaining about now?" asked Becky, sidling up to us. Becky is always trying to suck up to Heidi. It really galls her that Heidi likes us Pinecones more than her.

Heidi wasn't paying much attention to me or Becky. She was looking around the gym. The tall man standing behind the judges' table was pacing back and forth like a tiger. He was wearing a cheap straw cowboy hat. I hate men who try to look like cowboys.

"I wish he'd stand still," I said. "He's making me nervous."

"Who is he?" asked Heidi. "He looks so familiar, but I can't place him."

"Who knows?" I said. "He's probably some witch Coach Miller hired to put a hex on the Pinecones."

"Lauren," said Heidi, laughing at me, "you know that's not true."

"Lauren's so silly," said Becky.

"You're right," I admitted. "Men can't be witches. It's a proven fact that male witches are called warlocks. I bet he's a warlock."

Heidi shook her head. "Cut it out," she chided me. "You're psyching yourselves up to lose. You can't let yourself be bothered by things you can't control."

"Yeah, you don't have to worry," I said. "Nobody's got a warlock putting a hex on you."

I was just kidding, but Heidi took me seriously. Heidi tends to take everything seriously, particularly competition. I don't.

Heidi was in the middle of a great comeback. When I met her, she weighed about seventy pounds, and she was in the hospital. She was about to quit gymnastics altogether. Then I got

10

her together with Patrick, and slowly she's begun to come back.

The next Atomic Amazon did an almost perfect Yamashita. Coach Miller threw his fist into the air. He looked over at the tall man, who jerked his chin down in appreciation. It was as if their team had already triumphed.

My first vault was lousy. I knew I had to score higher on my second or we'd have a disaster on our hands.

"This time," said Heidi, "just block everything out except you and the horse."

"Neigh!" I whinnied.

Heidi clucked disapprovingly. "Lauren, stop joking around," she said to me.

Patrick came up to us. "Lauren, are you getting final advice from the expert?" he asked. Patrick really respected Heidi. In some ways, she had almost become our assistant coach.

"Lauren's psyching herself into a tizzy over Coach Miller," said Heidi. Sometimes Heidi sounds like she's forty, not fourteen.

"Just go full out," said Patrick. "It's what you do best."

I knew what Patrick meant. Some kids are scared of running full speed, but speed is the key. I love to run fast.

I saluted the judge. She raised her pencil in the air to tell me she was ready. I blinked. Something was in my eye. I could feel it, but I didn't know what to do. I could call for a time-out, but this judge already had it in for me.

I blinked again and started my run. I hit the springboard, and my hands reached out for the horse, but my eye was tearing.

I could see Patrick moving toward me between the springboard and the horse. My hands were too close to my body. I didn't have any leverage to push myself up and out from the horse.

I arched my back and tried to force my body over the horse, but it was no good. I landed stomach-first on the mats on the other side. I forced myself to get to my feet and salute the judge again. Then I rubbed my eye.

Patrick walked onto the mat and came up to me. "Are you okay?" he asked.

"Something's in my eye," I said.

Patrick turned around.

The judge's score went up. It was 1.00.

At first I had a weird feeling I had actually gotten a ten for the first time in my life. Then I knew it was a 1.00. I couldn't believe it. I had loused up the vault, but I had gotten over the horse.

Patrick stared at the score also.

He went over to the judges' table. "Excuse me," he said. "Was there a mistake with the score?"

The judge tapped her pencil impatiently on the scorecard.

"No. Why?" she asked.

"A 1.00. That was a vault with high difficulty."

"Coach Harmon," said the judge in a loud, grating voice. She had one of those singsong voices that teachers often have. I think they must attend special classes to get them.

"Your gymnast fell on the landing. She had no pre-flight to speak of, and then, of course, you cost her nearly a point because I saw you get between the springboard and the horse."

"I could see that she was in trouble," argued Patrick.

"I had something in my eye," I explained.

"I assume your coach taught you the correct way to approach the judges and ask for a time-out," said the judge.

"Of course I did," sputtered Patrick. "But Lauren felt she had something to prove."

"That's not my problem," said the judge.

"It is when you insult my gymnast with a ridiculously low score," said Patrick.

The man in the cowboy hat was listening to every word. I wondered if he was the parent of one of the Atomic Amazons. I could feel his eyes on Patrick and me.

Patrick didn't back down. "There was no reason to humiliate my gymnast," he said.

"Coach Harmon," said the judge, "you know the rules. If you want to raise an objection, you can go through the proper channels."

"Don't ever humiliate one of my gymnasts again," said Patrick. I was proud of Patrick for standing up for me.

"Coach Harmon, is that a threat?" asked the judge.

Patrick just shook his head and guided me back to the bench. The man in the cowboy hat was staring at us both.

I Don't Like Cowboys

We never got a chance to catch up. I had known it in my heart. We went into the Amazons' dressing room, which is the best thing about their gym. It's part of a health club, and it's all pink with little alcoves with hair driers and mirrors.

"Don't worry," said Jodi as she was drying her hair. "We can beat them next time. We have two more meets with them."

"At least next time, maybe we'll start on even ground," said Ashley.

"Ashley, will you drop it?" said Darlene. "It's no good blaming Lauren. None of us performed well today."

"I did my best," whined Ashley.

"You didn't," said Cindi. "You fell off the beam

two times, and you looked like you were sleep-walking through your floor routine."

Cindi is really competitive. She hates to lose more than any of us, and none of us think losing is fun.

I twisted my neck. My shoulder was a little sore from where I had landed on my fall from the vault.

"Hey," I said, "let's not start picking on each other. What happend to that old Pinecone spirit?"

"It got run over by a bunch of Amazons," mumbled Jodi.

"Still, you were right," I said. "Next time, we'll get them. I just hope we don't get the same judge." We came out of the locker room. My parents were there, along with the parents of most of the other Pinecones. They were all talking to Patrick. Patrick saw us and left them and came over to us. I knew what he was going to say.

"Turn the page," I teased him. That's what Patrick always tells us to do after a loss.

"Yes, there's that," said Patrick. "But we're really going to have to work harder. There was a lot of sloppiness out there."

"We never really had a chance," Ashley muttered.

"I don't want that kind of talk," said Patrick. He looked over in the corner where the Atomic

16

Amazons were celebrating their victory. The judge that I hated was talking to them, too, along with the guy in the cowboy hat.

"Come on, girls," he said. "Let's go over and congratulate the Amazons."

"Oh, Patrick," I said. "I can't bear it. They're all so smug."

"Lauren," said Patrick, "you're coming."

"Better be careful, Lauren," Cindi said to me. "Patrick's in a lousy mood."

"It's all because of me," I said.

Cindi put her arm around me. "You're taking this a little too seriously," she said.

We walked over to the Atomic Amazons. "Congratulations," I said to the girl who had done the perfect Yamashita vault.

"You had a tough day," she said.

I smiled at her, pleased that she was nicer than I had expected.

Patrick was talking to Coach Miller, who was laughing when he introduced him to the guy in the cowboy hat.

"Who is he?" I asked the Atomic Amazon girl. "Is he somebody's parent?"

The girl shrugged. "He's some foreign coach. He's been hanging around the gym for the past couple of days. Coach Miller says that he's just a pest and to ignore him."

"Somebody should tell him to stand still during a meet," I said. "He really distracted me."

"Is that why you messed up?" asked the Atomic Amazon. I was no longer sure how nice she was.

"No," I admitted. "We all just had an off day."

She giggled. "Too bad your coach got himself all worked up," she said. "Our coach says that Patrick is an unprofessional hothead."

"Coach Miller doesn't know diddley-squat!" I said. Nobody could put Patrick down in front of me and get away with it.

Apparently I spoke louder than I knew. The entire area around us grew silent. Then I heard someone laughing. It was a big booming laugh. I turned around. I knew that my face was red.

It was the man in the cowboy hat, and he was laughing at me.

I don't like cowboys.

Bug? Did He Say Bug?

It is hard to get yourself psyched to go back to the gym after a bad loss. We'd had all weekend to think about it. We almost never have workouts on weekends.

My parents had driven me home after the meet. They knew how badly I had done, but they didn't think it should bother me. Mom and Dad are much prouder that I'm in the gifted and talented program at school than of the fact that I can do a complicated vault.

Neither Mom nor Dad are sports nuts. Dad is a high school principal, and he thinks sports get too much attention at his school. Mom is on the Denver city council, and she thinks there are a lot more important things in life than winning or losing a gymnastics meet. I guess in the larger scheme of things she's right, but it's hard to feel that way when you're the one who has lost.

On Mondays, I always go to the gym after school. That morning, I reached for the cereal box, and I winced.

"What's wrong?" asked Dad.

"It's nothing," I said. "It's my shoulder from where I fell on the vault. But it's not really hurt."

"Maybe you shouldn't do gymnastics today," Mom said.

"It's not hurt, just sore," I argued. "Patrick's taught us to know the difference."

"Another Patrick quotation for the day," teased Dad, who knows that I do repeat things Patrick says a lot. It's just because he makes sense.

"Well, it's true," I said. "Patrick doesn't want us to hurt ourselves. He's really careful."

"I know, honey, I know," said Mom. "Still, if you're overtired from your meet and you're sore, I think you should consider taking a break."

Mom grinned at me. I knew she was half kidding. We'd had this discussion in different versions lots of times before. Mom is always suggesting that perhaps I "take a break" from gymnastics. But we have a deal — as long as I keep up with my schoolwork I can go to the gym as much as I please. Even after a loss, the gym is still my favorite hangout place.

When I got to the gym after school, Heidi was already there, working with a special dance coach, Madame Maria. Heidi doesn't have to go to school. She takes correspondence classes so that she can work out almost full time.

Heidi waved to me from the bar where she was finishing her dance routine. "Remember, lift the head . . . lift the head," trilled Madame Maria. Madame Maria walks with a cane because of an old dance injury, and she has a thick Russian accent.

I went to the bar and began my own slow warm-ups. Heidi grinned at me. "You all recovered from the meet?" she asked.

"My shoulder's sore," I said.

"I meant your spirit, not your body," said Heidi.

The other Pinecones drifted in, and we began our warm-ups together.

Madame Maria stamped her cane on the ground. "Come on, Heidi," she commanded.

"Hey!" I said, looking up from my stretches. "What's *he* doing here?"

The man with the cowboy hat was over in the corner, sitting on a bench with Patrick. He had his hat in his hand, and he looked too big for the bench. He was older than I first thought, with gray hair at his temples. He and Patrick were talking very seriously.

"That's Dimitri Vickorskoff," said Heidi excitedly, and Heidi almost never shows emotion in her voice.

"Who?" I asked.

"He's the Hungarian coach. He was the mastermind behind the whole Hungarian gymnastics dynasty," said Heidi. "I thought I recognized him the other day."

"Heidi," trilled Madame Maria, "we are not here to waste time." She glanced over to where Patrick and the guy were talking.

Dimitri Vickorskoff looked up at her. Madame Maria gave him a haughty look.

"Dimitri Vickorskoff!" said Ashley with awe in her voice. "I've read about him. He's known as the genius of Budapest."

"One of the Atomic Amazons told me that he was just a plain pest," I said.

Just then, Patrick and the guy got off the bench and came over to Heidi and Madame Maria. Patrick gestured to the Pinecones to stop our warm-ups and join them.

"Girls, I have a thrill for you. I want you to meet Dimitri Vickorskoff. He has come to the United States looking for a job."

"Humph," sniffed Madame Maria. "I *already* know Dimitri."

Dimitri stuck his big hand out to Madame Maria. "You look full of vonder," said Dimitri.

22

"The English word is *wonderful*, Dimitri," said Madame Maria.

I looked from one to the other. Something was definitely going on between them, and it didn't seem like they were old friends.

"Dimitri and I were competitors against each other years and years ago, when I choreographed for the Russian team, and he was coach of the Hungarian team," said Madame Maria. "He was a very, very tough competitor."

"I vas not so tough," said Dimitri. He had a thick accent and it was kind of hard to understand him.

"Girls, I have some very exciting news for our gym. Dimitri will be staying here for a while, and he is going to help coach us. He's willing to teach me some of his techniques."

"You girls vill have to forgive my English," said Dimitri. "I learn your *Sesame Avenue*."

I giggled. Cindi poked me.

"That's okay," said Jodi quickly. "Our English isn't always too good around here, either." She shook hands with Dimitri. "I'm Jodi Sutton. I think you know my mom and dad." Jodi's mom used to be a world-class gymnast. She's a coach at Patrick's gym, but she's taking time off right now because she just had a baby.

"Yes, your mother vas an excellent gymnast," said Dimitri.

One by one the Pinecones introduced themselves. Ashley practically curtsied as if she were meeting royalty.

I got introduced last. "Ah," said Dimitri, "The little bug at the vault!"

"Excuse me?" I asked, but Dimitri had already turned to meet Heidi and Becky. Becky was gushing all over him. "It will be such an honor to work with you, sir."

"Bug?" I whispered to Cindi. "Did he say 'bug'?"

"I'm sure you heard it wrong," said Cindi. "Isn't this exciting?"

"Yeah, as exciting as cockroaches," I muttered.

Thrilling and Exciting

"All right, girls," said Patrick. "Dimitri is just going to watch today. I want to go over some of the mistakes we made in the meet."

"Right, like Lauren losing her cool in the warm-ups," squeaked Ashley. "You probably sure impressed Dimitri."

"Yeah, he thinks I'm a bug," I said.

"That's enough, Ashley," said Patrick. "As I said on Saturday, everybody was sloppy. We've got to start paying attention to the little details that add to your score. We're going to go back to fundamentals for the next couple of weeks. I want you to work hard at remembering to point your toes. . . ."

Ashley wasn't really paying attention to Patrick. She kept glancing over at the sidelines where Dimitri was pacing up and down. "It's so exciting to have him here," she said. "Is Dimitri going to teach the Pinecones, too, or just the advanced kids?"

"We haven't worked out exactly what he'll do," said Patrick, "but I'm sure he'll give the Pinecones some pointers."

"Madame Maria didn't seem too happy to see him," I said.

"Dimitri's a controversial character," said Patrick, "but the guy deserves a chance. He's had no help at all from the official gymnastics circles."

"Why did he leave Hungary if he's so famous?" I asked.

"The sports federations of the Eastern bloc countries are in trouble after all the changes going on over there," said Patrick. "A lot of Soviet and Eastern bloc coaches are looking for work."

"I think maybe he should have stayed in his own country," I said.

"Lauren," said Ti An, "you don't mean that."

I blushed. Ti An is Vietnamese, and her parents are immigrants. My dad's Hispanic. I guess I didn't have any right to say that Dimitri didn't belong here.

"I don't mean that he shouldn't be *here* in the United States, I just wish that he wasn't in our gym."

I watched as Dimitri was talking with his hands to Becky and Heidi. He was very distracting to watch. "Why does he have to wave his hands around so much?" I asked.

"Lauren, that's just his style," said Patrick. "He's a very emotional guy."

I narrowed my eyes. "What exactly did you mean when you said Dimitri was staying here?" I asked.

"Dimitri doesn't have a place to live, so I told him he could camp out on the sofabed in my office until he gets on his feet."

Dimitri's feet were encased in a pair of cheap cowboy boots. They were huge feet. I didn't like the idea of those big feet living in *my* gym.

"I don't get it," I complained. "If he's so famous, why did he end up in our gym and not some world-famous gym?"

I love the Evergreen Gymnastics Academy, but we are not exactly a luxurious gym. We're located in the suburbs of Denver in an old warehouse. Until Heidi started working out with us, nobody in the international gymnastics world had ever heard of Patrick and us. Why, if this coach was so famous, was he going to be working with Patrick instead of with somebody high up in the gymnastics coaching world, like Darrell Miller?

"I think some of the American coaches are afraid of the competition," said Patrick. "It just so happens that I think he could be a great help to Heidi and to the rest of us. I can learn a lot from him."

I didn't like Patrick sounding so respectful.

"I think he's *too* big for our gym," I said.

"Lauren, will you let me run my own gym?" demanded Patrick.

I bit my lip.

"Give Dimitri a chance," said Darlene. "I think it will be a thrilling experience for all of us."

I was hearing too much thrilling and exciting. I don't like to be *told* that something is thrilling and exciting. I'd rather find out for myself. It's like a teacher telling you that something is going to be "very interesting." It never is.

Splitting Up
the Pinecones

"Good noon," bellowed Dimitri as I walked into the gym. He was dressed in brand-new blue jeans with the crease still in them, and this time he was wearing a black Stetson hat.

"Afternoon," I said.

Dimitri grinned at me. "Thank you. You help my English. Now today, I help you. Go get changed. Today ve vill vork together. My new hat vill bring you luck. Do you like it?"

"It's quite something," I said.

"It's a present from your Patrick," said Dimitri. "I like it. It makes me look very long."

"Tall," I corrected. "And you are already tall."

Dimitri laughed as if I were making a big joke.

I pushed open the swinging door to the locker room.

"I can't stand the fact that that guy is everywhere," I said.

"What guy?" asked Cindi.

Darlene just grinned at me. "Dimitri. Lauren's complaining about Dimitri again."

"How can he not bother you?" I asked. "He's been hanging around for the past two weeks, watching everything we do."

"He's trying to learn English," said Darlene. "He speaks Hungarian, Russian, French, and German, but he says that English is the hardest."

"I think it's amazing how quickly he's picking it up," said Cindi.

"Well, I wish he'd stick to *Sesame Avenue*." I opened my locker and put on my leotard. "Now he's wearing a black Stetson. Patrick gave it to him as a present. Stetsons are expensive. Why is Patrick giving him a present? He's already letting him sleep here. I don't know why Patrick has to be so nice."

"It's because Patrick *is* nice," said Cindi. "I think it's kind of cute the way Dimitri wears western clothes. He wants to be so American."

"I think he looks like a clown, and I think he's taking advantage of Patrick," I said.

"Lauren, cool it," said Darlene.

"Mom said that Dimitri was famous for his terrible temper," said Jodi. "She said he even used to yell at the judges."

"You see," I said, "he's unpredictable. We can't have him coming to our matches and bothering the coaches."

Cindi started laughing. "What are you laughing at?" I asked her. Cindi knows me best of any of the Pinecones. She and I have been friends ever since kindergarten.

"You thought Patrick was wonderful when he yelled at the judge at our last meet. *You* even yelled at the judge. What's wrong with Dimitri yelling at a few judges? I think the judges should be shaken up every once in a while."

"Yeah, give Dimitri a chance," said Jodi. "So far he hasn't bothered us. He's been spending most of his time with Heidi and Becky."

"That's another thing I don't like," I said. "Patrick's been great for Heidi, and now Dimitri is putting his big foot in there. Who knows what could happen?"

"Would you stop predicting disaster and finish getting dressed?" teased Cindi. "We've got to get out to the gym."

Dimitri and Patrick were standing together near the vault. Heidi and Becky were sitting on the bench, relaxing. I knew that Dimitri had been working on a complicated vault with them all week.

Dimitri was making huge gestures with his hand, every once in a while pounding the horse for emphasis.

Patrick was nodding his head in agreement. I didn't like to see Patrick agreeing with everything that Dimitri said.

Patrick gestured for us to come over to the horse.

Dimitri was grinning like an idiot.

"Today, Dimitri wants to work on the vault with our best vaulters. Lauren, that means Dimitri wants to work with you, Becky, and Heidi."

I shook my head and folded my hands over my arms. "You've got to be kidding. I'm a Pinecone. I don't work out with those advanced kids."

"You are ready," said Dimitri, nodding his head up and down for emphasis.

I sighed. "Patrick, will you explain to Dimitri that I am a Pinecone? I don't work out with Becky."

Becky giggled. "I knew this was going to be a disaster," she said.

"Dimitri has been talking to me about challenging each of you," said Patrick. "He feels that the Pinecones are ready to be pushed. That means, Darlene, you'll be working out with the advanced team on your floor exercise and beam. Cindi, Ti An, and Jodi, we'll do some advanced exercises on the bars. Ashley, you're ready for some more complicated moves on the beam."

"But we're a team," I protested to Patrick.

"A team that lost," Dimitri reminded us.

I wanted to murder him.

"You'll still be a team," said Patrick.

"But we always do everything together," I objected.

Dimitri was shaking his head. "Come, my little bug," he said. "Ve try my vay."

"Patrick," I wailed.

"We're trying it his way," he said.

I couldn't believe it. This Dimitri character was splitting up the Pinecones. I was going to have to find a way to stop him.

7

A Contest of Vill

"Now, Lauren," said Dimitri, rolling the *r* in my name. "Heidi knows, of course, the vault I teach you. Becky has most of it down. But you, ve vill start with the basic Vickorskoff."

"You want me to learn *what*?" I exclaimed. I was sure that I had misunderstood him. "You mean the Yamashita vault. That's the most difficult vault I can do."

Dimitri was shaking his head. He had moved the springboard over to a pile of mats that stood about a foot high.

"He said the Vickorskoff," said Heidi to me. "After all, he invented it."

"He's got to be kidding," I said. "He's nuts." Until Heidi started working out at the gym, the

34

only place I had seen the Vickorskoff vault was on television.

It's a vault that starts with the gymnast jumping onto the horse backward. Instead of running and hitting the board, you do a cartwheel with a twist *onto* the board and then reach for the horse with your back to it.

"I don't have eyes in the back of my head," I said to Dimitri.

"Too much joking isn't good, my little bug," said Dimitri. I looked around for the other Pinecones. Together, we would have made mincemeat out of Dimitri. The *best* thing about the Pinecones was the proven fact that we believed joking was good for us.

"I wasn't joking," I said sullenly to Dimitri. "I *know* this vault is too hard for me."

Dimitri seemed to have very selective hearing. He pretended I hadn't said anything.

"Come, I show you how I teach all the little ones."

I couldn't believe it. Dimitri, this six-foot-four giant in cowboy boots, started to run down the runway and did a cartwheel, landing on the board with such force that the *boing!* echoed throughout the gym, then he threw himself flat on his back on the mats. The force of his weight was so huge that the mats kind of slithered out from under him, helter-skelter.

I couldn't stop laughing. Heidi was giggling, too.

Dimitri waved to us from his position on his back. "You see, that's how you learn not to be afraid of hitting the horse backvard. Now you vill try it."

I was holding my hand over my mouth, trying to stop giggling at the ridiculous Dimitri trying to demonstrate the vault.

"You don't think I'm a butterfly," said Dimitri. "A frog can be a gymnast, too."

"Am I a frog or a bug?" I asked him.

"No jokes," said Dimitri. "I vill tell you a story. Vonce, I had to pass test in gymnastics. Every time I hung upside down in the rings, I vould get seasick." Dimitri held his stomach to show us how he felt.

"It vass big challenge to me. I teach myself. Even though I am big giant, I learn gymnastics. I teach myself, and that's how I learn to teach others. From a little seasick."

"Isn't he something?" said Heidi as Dimitri went to set the mats back up. "The more I learn about him, the more impressed I am."

"You're impressed with that kind of talk?" I asked Heidi.

"He's a winner," said Heidi. Her dark eyes were bright.

"Patrick's a winner, too," I said.

36

"I know," said Heidi, but she said it as if she were just trying to placate me. "But I need to be pushed. If I'm really going to make a comeback, I've got to get serious."

"Patrick's serious," I said. "He's serious and funny at the same time. That's what's so wonderful about Patrick."

Heidi just shook her head impatiently. "You don't understand," she whispered.

"Of course she doesn't," sneered Becky. "Lauren's a Pinecone. She doesn't realize what an opportunity's fallen in our laps by having Dimitri."

Heidi nodded. I didn't mind Becky saying something stupid and pompous. That's her personality. But I sure minded the fact that Heidi agreed with her.

If it was a contest of "vill" that Dimitri wanted, I would give it to him.

8

Too Much Goo in It

Dimitri finished piling the mats back together. He moved the springboard in front of them. "Too much talking," he said. "Ve are about to be serious. Lauren, you start with something easy. A roundoff onto the mats. Ve pretend the board is the horse and you fall over backvard onto the mat. Ve run just like a real vault. Okay!"

I felt a wave of relief. I thought he was going to insist on doing something much more difficult. A roundoff I can do. It's just a cartwheel with a half twist on it. I would do the best one that I knew how.

I started my run and flung my hands over my head. I really jumped high. I landed on the mats feet first, in a much better position than Dimitri had. I jumped up. Patrick would have been smiling at me.

Dimitri was just shaking his head. "No . . . too many steps. How many steps you usually run for a vault?"

I shrugged. "As many as it takes to get me down the runway," I said. "Patrick says I have a very explosive run."

Dimitri shook his head as if he wasn't very impressed. "Come." He took my hand and started counting off in his strange accent the number of steps that he wanted me to take for every vault. One . . . two . . . sixty-four, sixty-five . . . seventy-one.

"There!" he said triumphantly. "Every time you run seventy-von steps. Now try roundoff again, and this time you do exactly seventy-von steps before you round off."

I scrunched up my eyes. "You mean count the exact number of steps each time? That's silly. I'm a natural vaulter."

Dimitri shook his head. "No, no," he said. "No such thing. Ve vork and vork and then it becomes like nature. Now, do it."

I walked to the start of the runway. I was so busy counting in my head that when I finally got to seventy-one, I had forgotten to hurdle to start my roundoff. I tripped into the mats.

"That was step seventy-two," I joked.

"Again," said Dimitri without cracking a smile. "Do it again." Meanwhile, he had Heidi and Becky adding complicated half twists to their approach. Heidi looked like she was having fun. Becky's face was red, and she looked tired. My work was so boring I felt I was going to scream.

I did it again . . . and again . . . and again. I spent the entire two-hour workout counting out steps and rounding off onto the mats.

Finally he said, "Von more time."

I rolled my eyes. "At last," I sighed to Heidi. "If he said 'again' von more time I was going to brain him."

Heidi didn't crack a smile. She was breathing hard from her workout, but her eyes were constantly on Dimitri.

"Lauren!" shouted Dimitri. "Von more time."

I started down the runway counting in my head. This time I got the rhythm right, and I did as good a roundoff as I had done at the beginning of the workout. At least I'd be ending on a high note.

Dimitri nodded. "Betterrrr," he said. "Now, von more time and this time try to point your toes."

"Huh!" I exclaimed. "That *was* my 'von more time.' In English, one more time means that's the last one."

"Enough joking," said Dimitri. "Thank you for correcting my English. Von more time."

"Is he for real?" I asked Heidi as I trotted back down the runway.

"In Dimitri language," laughed Heidi, "one more time is just the beginning."

"This has got to be a joke," I exclaimed.

"It's not," said Becky. "He says that just to torture you."

Dimitri made me do twenty "von more times." I was so exhausted and bored I wanted to scream. Finally he said. "Goo-ood . . . a beginning. Ve do this again tomorrow."

Dimitri's "good" has too much "goo" in it for my taste.

9

Lazy and a Fool

I was drenched in sweat. My body ached. I stretched out on the mats piled high at the side of the gym and closed my eyes. I was sure I was going to hear "von more time" in my sleep.

"Lauren," I heard Patrick's voice. I love the sound of his voice. It's warm and gentle, and it doesn't sound anything like Dimitri's.

I opened my eyes.

"Are you okay?" he asked.

I sat up and twisted my neck around. I could hear crinkly noises. "I don't like it when my neck talks," I said.

Patrick laughed. I like to make him laugh. I sat up and watched Dimitri putting Heidi through her paces. His loud voice seemed to bounce from the ceiling.

"How was your first workout with Dimitri?" Patrick asked.

"I think it should be my last," I said. "He's not a good coach for me."

Patrick frowned. "Lauren," he said, "this is a wonderful opportunity for you. You have to seize it."

"*You're* a wonderful coach," I said. "I don't need him."

Patrick was watching Dimitri. "I love the way he works so intensely," he said.

"All he knows how to say is 'von more time,' " I complained.

"I don't like you making fun of his accent," said Patrick. "It's rude."

"Sorry," I muttered, but he could tell I didn't mean my apology.

"Lauren," warned Patrick in that serious voice he uses when he has something really important to say. "There is a reason why I want you to work with Dimitri."

"What is it, then?" I asked. I was feeling kind of hurt that Patrick had foisted me off on Dimitri. I was also kind of angry with him, and a little nervous at what he was going to say.

"Dimitri is very demanding, but he is also a great coach, better than I am — "

"I don't think he's so great," I interrupted, "and nobody's better than you."

"Well, Dimitri is. I hope I'll be as great as he is someday, but right now, he's the one who has coached a whole generation of Hungarian gymnasts to world titles and Olympic medals, and I've decided he has something to offer you that I can't."

"I don't know what," I complained. "I do fine with just you coaching me."

"You don't like it that he always asks you to repeat a move, but that's just what you need." Patrick tried to explain. "I realized that I let you off sometimes because I don't want to be too hard on you, but you could really do a lot better. Sometimes we all need shaking up."

That made it even worse! Now Patrick was telling me that I was lazy, and he was getting this ornery old Dimitri to get on my case because he didn't want to bother to do it himself.

"If that's all it is, I'll try harder, Patrick, I promise. I just don't think Dimitri is going to help me."

"But I do," Patrick said in his "coach" voice that tells you this is not something he will discuss or argue about, but you must just do it. Everyone always does — I always do. But this time I couldn't.

"Well, I don't want to learn from Dimitri. And

you're absolutely wrong. There is no better coach than you."

Patrick shook his head. "Lauren, I'd be a fool if I thought that, just like you're a fool if you don't see what a fantastic opportunity this is."

"Great. First I'm lazy, and now I'm a fool," I muttered.

"Dimitri is going to be good for all of us," said Patrick. "You'll see."

I just glared at him.

10

Dracenstein

I ran into the locker room and just sank down on the floor next to my locker. Sitting on the bench would have required too much effort.

Darlene came in and took off the wrist bands she had been wearing. They were soaked through with sweat. One by one the Pinecones filed into the locker room. All of them looked exhausted, as if they'd been hit by a freight train. I knew all about the freight train — its name was Dimitri Vickorskoff.

"I just had my first mini-session with Dimitri on my floor routine," Darlene said. "I feel like I've been hit by a cyclone. How was he on the vault?"

"How was he on vault?" I shrieked. "That's like asking how Dracula is at giving neck massages."

Darlene giggled.

"I'm not kidding," I said. "Think about it. Dracula was tall. Dimitri's tall. Dracula was from one of those countries over there. I think Dimitri definitely, definitely could be Count Dracula. Look at the way he tries to count: von . . . two . . ."

"I think you're the one who's been watching too much *Sesame Street*," said Darlene. "Your brain's turning to mush." She smiled at me tolerantly. She was sure I was just horsing around.

"I'm serious, Darlene. Dimitri's a tyrant. And Patrick."

"What's wrong with Patrick?" asked Jodi.

"Patrick is totally hoodwinked by this guy," I said.

Cindi shook her head. "Lauren, come off it. I thought it was kind of exciting working with Dimitri." She looked at her hands. They were very red, and she had a new rip on her palm.

"He worked you on bars, didn't he?" I asked her. Bars are the most dangerous event that we do. If you don't hit the bars just right, you can really hurt yourself.

"Yeah," said Cindi. "He's so tall that when he spots you he makes you feel real secure. It's not that he taught me anything so different. It's just that he wants every detail to be perfect."

I stared at her. My best friend was fooled by Dimitri, too.

I twisted my neck and could hear it crinkle. "Cindi, the guy's got you hypnotized. You and Patrick."

"Hey," said Jodi, "I agree with Cindi. I think he's kind of cool, too."

"He makes me tired," said Ti An.

"Good," I said. "At least you agree with me."

"Tired in a good way," said Ti An. "I think he's very interesting."

"Yeah, that's what they said about Frankenstein when the good doctor invented him. He's going to be very interesting."

Ti An giggled. "First he's Dracula. Now he's Frankenstein. Make up your mind."

"He's Dracenstein," I said.

"Lauren, chill out on this," said Darlene as she started to get undressed.

"Chill out?" I said. "I thought you were the one who agreed with me. You said you felt like a cyclone hit you."

"I didn't say that being hit by a cyclone was a bad thing," said Darlene. She laughed. "Maybe we needed to be hit by a cyclone. We needed something after our last loss to the Amazons."

"That's what I think," said Ashley excitedly. "I think the man's a real genius."

I made a face but didn't say anything.

Heidi and Becky came into the locker room together. Heidi looked as cool as a cucumber.

Becky looked a little bedraggled. Her hair was sticking to her forehead, and her eyes looked dazed. She sank down to the floor beside me and twisted her neck. I could hear it crackle.

"That guy's a monster," she said.

Heidi's lips were in a thin line, the way they are when she's angry.

"Will you stop complaining?" said Heidi impatiently.

Becky just rolled her eyes. "If I hear that Hungarian madman say 'von more time' one more time . . ." Becky did a perfect imitation of Dimitri. I laughed.

Becky crossed her eyes as she looked at me. "I suppose you're going to tell me he's a genius, too," she said.

I swallowed hard. I could see the other Pinecones staring at me.

"Lauren agrees with you," said Ashley prissily. "She called Dimitri Dracula."

"Actually, she called him Dracenstein," piped up Ti An.

"That's a good one, Lauren," said Becky. "Dimitri Dracenstein. I'm sure that's got to be his real name."

I inched a little away from Becky, still finding it hard to get used to the idea that Becky and I agreed about anything.

Heidi had her hands on her hips. "I can't be-

49

lieve you guys," she said. "You've been handed the opportunity of a lifetime on a silver platter, and all you can do is complain."

"Hey, wait a minute," Cindi protested. "Be fair. Not all the Pinecones are complaining."

"Yeah," I admitted, feeling a little creepy. "It's only me."

Heidi just shook her head at me. "You guys," she repeated.

11

A Conspiracy

I spent an entire two weeks simply doing a roundoff onto the springboard. I was bored. Dimitri didn't give me much encouragement. I never felt as if I was doing it right.

Patrick let Dimitri have his way. I knew it wouldn't do me any good to complain to Patrick. Every day Patrick stood by Dimitri's side with a clipboard in his hand. I don't know what Patrick thought he could be learning except how to say "one more time" with a Hungarian accent.

Then one day I came into the gym and Dimitri wasn't there. Patrick was setting up a deck of mats at vault height. I looked around the gym.

Blessedly, there was no six-foot-four Hungarian lurking around. It was just Patrick.

I put down my gym bag and hurried through my warm-ups. Becky was just finishing hers. Patrick caught me out of the corner of his eye. "Lauren," he said, "do those stretches one more time."

"Agghhh, it's catching, the dread Dracenstein disease. You've caught it from the mad Hungarian."

Becky laughed loudly.

Patrick gave me a warning look. "Sorry," I said quickly. "I was just making a joke."

"I don't like those kind of jokes in my gym," said Patrick.

"Oh, Patrick, lighten up," said Becky. "Lauren was just being funny. Where is the mad Hungarian today?"

Somehow when Becky said "mad Hungarian," it didn't sound very nice at all.

"He had to go to the immigration office to try to straighten something out," said Patrick. "He should be here soon. He told me what he wants you to do. You'll be starting a new drill."

"Patrick," I complained, "you're the boss. You're the one who should be deciding on our drills. Not Dimitri. I don't get it."

Patrick sighed. "Lauren, we've been over this before. I don't want to hear any more about it."

"He's hypnotized by this guy," Becky whispered to me.

I nodded. Then I realized what I was doing — agreeing with Becky again.

"You were the one who thought it was a great honor to be working with him," I whispered back to her.

"That was before I began hearing 'von more time' in my sleep," whispered Becky.

"Girls," said Patrick, "stop talking."

That was another thing. Patrick never used to mind when we whispered while we were waiting. Now he did — just because Dimitri didn't like chatting while we were working out. It seemed to me that Patrick was beginning to sound like a broken record. It was always "Dimitri this" and "Dimitri that."

"Okay, Lauren," said Patrick, "I want you to do a roundoff back handspring up to the mats, snap down to your feet, and then punch up onto the stack of mats."

"Patrick, you've got to be kidding," I said. "This is sounding like a tumbling routine, not a vault. I've got to practice on the horse. It's a proven fact that since Dimitri's been teaching me this silly vault, I haven't even touched a horse."

"And you won't until you finish this drill," said Patrick.

"That's really going to impress the Atomic Amazons," I said. "I'll just tell the judges, 'Excuse me, I don't do vaults anymore. I just do pieces of them onto mats.' "

Patrick put his hands on his hips. "Lauren, I've had it with your insubordination," he said. "Make up your mind. Are you going to do the drill?"

I didn't wait to hear the "or else" in Patrick's voice.

"I'll do it," said Becky. "I'm just glad for the chance to work with you and not Dimitri."

"Becky, Lauren, I don't want any more of your lip on this," said Patrick. He sounded very angry.

I shuffled my feet. Becky and I looked at each other. I think she was as surprised as I was by the fact that we were being lumped together.

"We're sorry, Patrick," we said in unison. We looked at each other again. It was a very weird sensation to feel in synch with Becky.

"Okay, Lauren, go for it," said Patrick. I ran toward the mats and did a roundoff back handspring, reaching behind my head for the stack of mats, but I missed them and ended by falling backwards onto the mats.

"It's a lot harder than it looks," I admitted to Patrick.

He smiled at me. "You'll get it. Try again."

I ran back to the wall. It was funny. Patrick could tell me to try it again, and it didn't bother me at all. If Dimitri had said it, I'd be literally *off* the wall.

Becky started her run. She did it much better than I had. She had a lot of speed on her takeoff, and it took her up and over the pile of mats.

"No, no," I heard a voice. "Becky, your head vas not in line vith your trunk." Dimitri was back.

Patrick looked at Dimitri. "I didn't catch that," he said.

"Yaw, Becky, your head must not flop around. You can hurt yourself that way. Keep it straight."

"Here, Dimitri, you take over," said Patrick. "How did it go at the immigration office?"

"Aw, awful," said Dimitri. "If you vant to know vat it vas like in Hungary under the Communists, go stand in line at your immigration office."

Becky wasn't interested in Dimitri's problems. "You know, Patrick, that felt very good. I think I did fine."

"No, no . . . the head vas wrong," said Dimitri flatly. "You try it again, after Lauren."

"Go, Lauren," said Patrick.

But Becky wasn't finished. "Look, I'm getting pretty tired of being told it's wrong every time I do it."

"Then do it right," said Dimitri. "Lauren — "

"You don't know what you're talking about,"

interrupted Becky. "You just came from the immigration office. You're not even an American."

"Becky," snapped Patrick. He sounded absolutely furious. I don't think I've ever heard him that angry. "Apologize and then leave this gym. I want you to go home and think about what you said. I don't *ever* want to hear that kind of talk."

The gym became completely silent. I bit my lip. I couldn't stop fidgeting. Becky was being kicked out.

Becky came back to where I was standing. Her head was down, but her neck was bright red with embarrassment.

"Becky," said Patrick, "I didn't hear your apology."

"I'm sorry, Dimitri," Becky shouted. Then she muttered to me. "You and me, we'll figure out a way to get rid of that Hungarian."

I started to shake my head. The last thing that I really wanted was for Patrick to think that I could be as nasty as Becky.

I started my run for the mats. Patrick stopped me. "Lauren, if I hear any more backtalk from you about Dimitri, you're next."

I grimaced.

How in the world had I ended up in a conspiracy with Becky?

He's Destroying Our Gym

Becky was allowed to come back the next day. Around Patrick she was a little subdued, but I knew that she hadn't changed her mind about Dimitri. The worst thing was that she was sure I agreed with her. I no longer knew what I thought. All I knew was that ever since Becky had discovered that I was just about her only ally in the gym, she had started searching me out like a heat-seeking missile.

Patrick called a gym meeting on Thursday. "I've got a few announcements that I want to go over," he said.

"I hope it's just for people *really* with the gym," whispered Becky. She nudged me with her elbow. I wished she'd stop doing that.

"What did you say?" Patrick asked.

"Nothing," grumbled Becky.

"All right, girls," said Patrick. "Do your warm-ups and then meet Dimitri and me over at the mats by the floor exercise."

"I hate the sound of 'Dimitri and me,' " I muttered as Patrick moved off to talk to Dimitri.

"We've got to figure out a way to make sure Patrick understands that Dimitri does not belong with us," whispered Becky.

I didn't answer her. I was thankful when Becky took off for the mats at the far end of the room.

"What are you and Becky up to now?" Darlene asked me as we started our stretches.

"Nothing," I said.

"Becky and Lauren *have* gotten mighty chummy lately," said Jodi.

"It does seem to be a proven fact that suddenly Becky is your great new friend," said Cindi.

"She's *not* my great new friend," I said. "It's not my fault Patrick forced me to learn this new vault with her. If it's anybody's fault that I've been spending time with Becky, it's Patrick's."

"Oh, right," said Cindi, sarcastically. "I can't believe you're blaming Patrick."

"At least she's not blaming Dimitri," said Jodi. "Lately that's all you've been doing."

"Hardly all," I said. I could feel myself getting

hot. Becky had been disgusting in her cracks about Dimitri. I *hated* the idea that my teammates thought I was as bad as she was. "I've been working mighty hard."

"Yeah, mighty hard at complaining," said Cindi.

"I can't believe you're saying that," I protested. "In fact, it's the exact opposite," I said. "I've never worked so hard in my life."

"Or complained about it more," said Cindi.

"Yeah, well, you're not working so intensely with Dimitri," I countered. "He's helping you on the bars, but he's teaching me something totally new."

"And you're lucky," said Cindi. "I can't wait until Dimitri teaches me a new routine. He said that next month he's going to work out a new drill for me."

"Next month?" I blurted out. "Does that mean that Dimitri is going to stick around forever?"

"If he does, we'll be lucky," said Darlene.

"They've all been brainwashed," Becky whispered to me. I wished she would shut up.

Patrick blew his whistle. "Girls, I want you over here for our meeting," he said.

Dimitri was sitting cross-legged in the middle of the mats, grinning like the Cheshire cat from *Alice's Adventures in Wonderland*. He seemed to have no idea that he was causing so much trouble.

"Dimitri's got some thoughts about our upcoming meet in a few weeks with the Amazons," said Patrick. "I thought we all should hear him."

"I have two thing to say," said Dimitri.

"That means two hundred," Becky whispered to me. I couldn't not giggle. Cindi gave me a dirty look. But I knew exactly what Becky meant. Dimitri would never say just two things.

"Ve vant to throw a little scare into those Amazons," said Dimitri. "This means that ve don't go to the competition just to show up. Ve go to vin."

I looked down at the edge of the mat where I was sitting. I had a horrible sinking feeling that I knew what Dimitri might have in mind.

"There's no way that I am ready to do that new vault," I blurted out.

"Yes, yes," said Dimitri. "But ve vill put a scare into them."

I stared at him. Sometimes when Dimitri said, "yes, yes," I wasn't sure whether he really meant yes or if he meant "no, no."

Dimitri hadn't even let me try the vault on the horse. All I did day after day was work on his two drills up onto the mats.

"You vill see," he said now. "It vill all come together."

60

"Yeah, but it's not going to come together for this meet," I said. I considered adding "or in this lifetime," since I really didn't think that I would *ever* learn the Vickorskoff vault.

"No," said Dimitri. "But *they* von't know it. Ven ve go to the varm-ups, you von't even touch the vault. You and I vill vork on the sidelines. I vill stack up the mats, just like ve do here, and they vill see you doing these drills. In their coach's mind, he vill be vondering, Vhat is Dimitri up to? He can't really have that little bug do the Vickorskoff vault, can he? He vill be nervous, and his little Amazons vill be nervous."

I had a hard time listening to anything Dimitri had to say after he called me a little bug again. If anything annoyed me, it was being known as "Dimitri's little bug."

"Everybody," said Dimitri, waving his hands in front of my face, "all my little bugs vill have a different spirit. You vill valk in with confidence."

"Dimitri, we're Pinecones, not bugs," I said.

Dimitri just nodded happily.

"Okay," said Patrick, "now we will have a serious practice."

"One more thing," said Dimitri.

Becky and I glanced at each other. "I told you," mouthed Becky.

Dimitri whispered something to Patrick. Patrick nodded. "You tell them," said Patrick.

"You are not working hard enough," said Dimitri. "To really vin, ve have to show vill. The meets are alvays held on Saturdays, yet you never practice on Saturdays. This is wrong. You must vork harder than ever on Saturdays. From now on, on Saturdays ve have two-a-day practices, since that's the day you vill vork hard on a meet."

"But . . . but," sputtered Darlene, "Saturday is the only day we have off when we don't have a meet."

"Wrong, wrong," said Dimitri. "Is not good to have Saturday off? No school. It's a perfect vork day."

"Saturday's Darlene's shopping day," teased Becky. Everybody knows that Darlene loves to shop.

"It's not just that," said Jodi. "Saturday's the only day we get to goof off."

"Good off?" asked Dimitri. "No, no, it's not good to be off. It's better to be on. Then you vill be hot, hot, hot for the meet."

"Good off," repeated Jodi, shaking her head.

"Enough, girls," said Patrick. "I don't want to hear any complaints about the Saturday practices. I think what Dimitri says makes sense. We're going to have to work extra hard to try to catch the Amazons. This is where we get serious."

"Get serious," muttered Jodi. "Two-a-day Saturday practices — I can't believe it."

"I told you Dimitri was destroying our gym," said Becky. She sounded very smug. For once the others didn't argue with her.

13

Mighty Strange

"Is there a meet today?" asked my father. Dad is an early riser. I'm not. Getting up and dressed by eight o'clock on Saturday morning is *not* my idea of fun.

I grunted. I wasn't in the mood to talk. I was still a little sore from the previous day's workout. Ever since Dimitri had come to the gym, I had discovered muscles I didn't even know I had. And every time I discovered a new muscle, I seemed to discover a new place to ache.

Dad glanced at our meet schedule that was posted on our refrigerator. He tries to make all of my meets, even though when I first started gymnastics he thought it was a waste of time.

"You don't have a meet for three weeks," said

Dad. "What are you doing in your gym clothes?"

"Saturday workouts," I said. "We've got one in the morning and one in the afternoon. It's the new regime."

"The new coach," said Dad, pouring me some orange juice. I gulped it gratefully. Dad had heard my complaints about Dimitri before.

"The Hungarian monster," I said. "All he knows is work. He's taking all the fun out of gymnastics."

Dad took a sip of his orange juice. "You didn't have much fun losing to the Amazons," he said. "Maybe at the next meet you'll finally show them."

I shook my head. "That's not the game plan," I said. "At our next meet, we're just supposed to scare the Amazons."

"And how are you going to do that?" Dad asked.

"We should probably all put on Dracenstein masks," I said. "That's about the only thing that will really scare the Amazons." I giggled. "You know, that's not a bad idea. Maybe it'll scare Dimitri away."

"Lauren," warned Dad, "I don't think you're giving this Dimitri a fair chance. If Patrick says he's good, you can probably learn a lot from him."

"Dad," I exploded, "if I hear that line one more time, I'm going to — "

"Going to what?" asked Dad softly.

I didn't have an answer.

"Is this Dimitri fellow doing something that really bothers you?" Dad asked. He sounded concerned.

I bit my lip. If I wanted to get rid of Dimitri I could make something up right now that would really get him in trouble. The problem was that I would have to make it up. Dimitri was a pest from Budapest, but he really hadn't done anything wrong. And I still felt uneasy about Becky's remarks.

"All he does is work us too hard," I said. "We're not just having Saturday workouts, we're having two a day!"

"That's a lot," said Dad. "Are you improving?"

I shrugged. "I can't tell. He's teaching me a new vault, but I haven't even tried to put it all together yet. 'Not ready yet,' is all Dimitri can say."

"He sounds like he's pretty careful," said Dad. "I don't want you taking too many risks."

I shook my head. "Risks? Wait till you see the Vickorskoff vault that he wants me to do. I would have never tried it in a million years! It's for kids way more advanced than I am."

Dad frowned. "Maybe this guy is pushing you too hard. I don't want you to do anything that's above your head. Perhaps I should talk to Patrick about it."

Mom came into the breakfast nook. She had been on the phone, even though it was before eight o'clock on Saturday morning. One thing I can say about politicians like Mom, besides the fact that they work hard, is that they spend all their time on the phone. Mom once talked on the phone so much she got a rash on her chin.

"Hi, honey," she said. She glanced at the refrigerator. "You don't have a meet today that I forgot about, do you?"

Mom looked guilty. She tries to get to all my meets, but sometimes she's too busy.

"Relax, Mom," I said. "I explained to Dad. It's not a meet. We're having Saturday practices, now. Another one of Dimitri's great ideas."

"Saturday practices?" repeated Mom. "Will that leave you enough time for homework?"

"Lauren's worried about this new Romanian coach that Patrick's got."

"He's not Romanian. He's Hungarian," I said.

"He's used to working with girls like Heidi," said Dad. "He's got Lauren trying things that are way over her head."

"I didn't say that," I protested.

Mom poured herself a cup of coffee and sat down. "I don't like the sound of this," she said. "You've been awfully tired lately."

"And sore," added Dad.

"I'm not that sore," I protested. I hate it when

my parents get on a tear like this.

Mom nodded. "It's true, Lauren. You've been sleeping like a log lately, and you've been complaining that you hurt."

"It's a good hurt, not a bad hurt," I said.

Dad stared at me.

"Well, gymnasts know," I said. "I know the difference between when I'm injured and when I'm just sore 'cause I've been working out."

"But now Saturday workouts," said Mom.

"Twice a day," said Dad.

"That sounds like way too much," said Mom. "It might be fine for someone like Heidi — it's her whole life — but not for you, Lauren."

"I didn't say it was too much," I complained. "My schoolwork's fine."

"Yes," said Dad, "but will you be able to keep it up when you're working this hard?"

"You worried about that when I first started gymnastics, and my grades went up," I argued. It was true. I've never had trouble in school, but since I've started gymnastics, I seem to concentrate better. I have so little time to waste that when I do my homework, I'm really there.

Dad was still frowning. "Still, maybe Mom or I should talk to Patrick. This Dimitri character might not be good for you. Perhaps Patrick doesn't realize how tired you are."

"For goodness' sake!" I was shouting now. "I'm not tired. I'm wide awake!"

Mom and Dad stared at me. "Please," I begged them, "let me handle this. I don't want you to talk to Patrick."

"Why?" Mom asked.

I didn't have a good answer. It was *mighty* strange. If Cindi and the other Pinecones had heard me, they wouldn't have believed it. Here I finally had a chance to try and get rid of Dimitri, and I didn't want my parents interfering. I just knew that I didn't.

14

Not a Flower — a Flier

I went into the locker room feeling a little confused, but at least I was wide awake. That's more than I could say for most of the other Pinecones.

I put on my leotard quickly. "Hey, Lauren," said Darlene with a yawn. "You seem unusually chipper."

"I can't believe that he's really making us do this," said Cindi. "Saturday workouts when we don't even have a meet."

"I told you," taunted Becky. "Lauren and I have been telling you guys all month that he was a monster. But no-o-o-o."

"Dracenstein," said Cindi. "Isn't that what you call him, Lauren?"

"It was a joke," I said.

"Yeah, but sometimes jokes tell the truth," said Ti An seriously.

I didn't have any answer to that. We went out into the gym. The early morning light came through the skylights, making the gym look a lot brighter than it did in the afternoon when we usually showed up after school.

"Good morning!" boomed out Dimitri. "This morning ve vork, right?"

"How can he be so cheery in the morning?" muttered Darlene.

"Warm up," said Patrick. "Warm up quickly, girls. Dimitri has a full schedule."

"Today ve do rotations," said Dimitri. "Boom, boom, boom. Some of you vill start on bars, then vault, tumbling, and beam. Everybody vill do everything. All four events, just like meet. Then ve do it again this afternoon. No talking."

Patrick was sipping a cup of coffee, watching Dimitri.

"Patrick," said Dimitri, "you spot them on bars. I'll vork on the vault and tumbling." Dimitri clapped his hands. "Okay, goo-ood . . . now ve start."

I went to work on the bars first. My bar routine was pretty difficult. I chalked up and grabbed the bar. I did a free hip circle on the low bar and then sailed for the high bar. I felt stronger than I ever had. I was right on the money.

"Yeah!" I shouted to Patrick. Patrick shook his head. "It's good, but you're not swinging high enough when you go for the high bar. And point your toes."

I frowned. "Hey!" I said. "It felt good."

"It shouldn't just *feel* good," said Patrick. "It's got to *look* good."

I stared at him. "Okay," I said, "I'll try it again."

"Good," said Patrick, but I thought I heard him kind of growl it out, like Dimitri's "goo-ood." I did it again. This time I concentrated on pointing my toes. I could tell that the routine was better.

"One more time," said Patrick. He winked at me.

"When Dimitri says that, it means the workout is half over," I teased.

I did my bars routine again and again. Normally I would have done my bar routine once or twice. Now I did it six times. Then I went to warm up on the beam and did eight beam routines, and I still had vault and floor routines left.

By the time I got to the vault, I had been working for nearly an hour and a half. It was hard on my body because Patrick and Dimitri didn't want us to slack off on one event just to save up strength for the others. We were working so hard that none of us wanted to talk. Every once in a while if somebody landed a particularly good routine, we'd shout for one another. Dimitri approved of cheering each other on; he just didn't like chitchat.

Finally it was time for the vault. I went over to the pile of mats, sure that we were going to do one or the other of our drills.

Instead, Dimitri had pulled the horse next to the foam pit. "Now ve try to put the pieces together for real," he said.

I licked my lips. Dimitri put his arm around me. He looked me in the eye. "You're ready," he said. "I spot you."

I nodded. Somehow I knew that Dimitri wouldn't let me try it unless he really thought I could do it.

"You go down the runway, and you do the roundoff, just like you've done hundreds of times," said Dimitri. "Then you do a back handspring, and the horse is just vere the mats have been, hundreds of times. It's a piece of pie."

"Piece of cake," I corrected. I swallowed hard.

I walked back down the runway. Becky saw me. "No way are you ready to try this vault," she said. "He's going to kill you."

"Shut up, Becky," I said. I needed to concentrate. I didn't need her telling me that I couldn't do it.

I headed down the runway. I hit the springboard with my hands and punched up. Trying a new trick is scary. I didn't know where I was. I was upside down, going headfirst for the horse, but I stuck my hands out, the way I had for the mats, and the leather padded horse was there. Dimitri's hands were on the small of my back, giving me just a little push, and then I landed feetfirst into the foam pit.

"All right!" I yelled. Dimitri was nodding his head and grunting. He held his hand out to give me a hand up. Then he gave me a hug.

"So, my little bug's a real fighter," he said. "A little rooster."

"Was it good?" I asked him.

He shook his head. "No. The landing not goo-ood. Now ve start to vork on the landing. You should go blam. Fasterr, fasterrr, powerfulllll, powerfulllllll! Blam! You are not a flower . . . you are a flier."

I started to giggle. Dimitri shook his head. "No, no, von more time . . . and this time, you must keep your head in line with your trunk."

Heidi was standing by the runway, ready to try her vault. Her eyes were beaming. "Way to go, Lauren!" she yelled. "I bet you never thought you'd be doing a Vickorskoff."

I grinned at her. Becky was frowning. "I thought you'd kill yourself," she muttered.

I rubbed my hands together. I wanted to try it again.

74

15

Some Kind of Monster

If we thought Saturday morning workouts were hard, we weren't prepared for the Saturday afternoon workouts. We took a break for lunch, and then we were back in the gym. Dimitri and Patrick were always waiting for us.

"I can't believe we're actually doing this," said Darlene.

"I tell you, the guy's a taskmaster," said Becky. "I read stories about him, before he ever came here. He's famous for turning his gymnasts into robots."

The rest of the Pinecones were listening to Becky. I put on my leotard. "Don't you agree, Lauren?" asked Becky.

I shrugged.

"Of course she agrees," said Cindi. "Lauren was the first one to tell us that Dimitri was a bad influence on Patrick. Maybe she was right all along."

Heidi came in. She looked as fresh and fit as if she hadn't done a workout.

"You kids had better shake a leg. They're waiting for you out there."

"Let the mad Hungarian wait," said Becky. "It's crazy to do two workouts on a Saturday."

Heidi thumped her gym bag down on the bench in front of the lockers. "Lauren," she shouted, "are you complaining about Dimitri again?"

"Uh . . . no," I found myself sputtering.

"You're nuts," said Heidi. "I saw what you did this morning. You wouldn't have come anywhere near doing the Vickorskoff if Dimitri hadn't pushed you."

"Yeah, but he pushes too hard," said Becky.

"You kids don't know how lucky you are," said Heidi. "I've seen the girls that Dimitri's trained at world competitions. They always look so ready and so confident. I've seen the Hungarian girls perform. This man knows what he's doing. You can't take that and just throw it away."

"But he's not our style," complained Becky.

"Your *style*?" sneered Heidi.

"Well, I won plenty of meets before Dimitri," said Becky.

"So did I," said Heidi. Ti An giggled. Heidi wasn't bragging. She was just stating a fact. Never in her lifetime would Becky win as many meets as Heidi. "And I know the difference that Dimitri can mean. That nine-tenths of a point that he can win for you, just by cleaning up your routine, can make all the difference in the world."

"Heidi," said Becky, "okay, maybe someone like Dimitri is good for you, but he doesn't belong coaching the Pinecones."

"You're just afraid of the competition, Becky," said Heidi. "Suddenly with Dimitri pushing them, it just might turn out that the Pinecones are a lot better than anybody thought."

Becky tittered as if that was the funniest thing she had ever heard.

"I'm not joking," said Heidi. She looked around the room at the Pinecones. "And as for you, you girls are fools if you fall for Becky's little ploy. She never wants you to be as good as you can be. Dimitri does."

Heidi flounced out of the locker room. The Pinecones all looked at one another.

"She's as nuts as Dimitri," said Becky. "The two of them are alike. They're both obsessed."

"I don't think Heidi's obsessed," I said. "She just wants to be a champion."

"Oh, come off it," said Becky. "You met her when she was in the loony bin."

"She *wasn't* in the loony bin," I protested. "She was in Children's Hospital because she was dehydrated and exhausted, and that's when she was with a California coach who pushed her too hard."

"Oh, and you don't think Dimitri pushes too hard?" said Becky sarcastically.

"Heidi sure doesn't look like she's suffering," I said. "She's never looked so good." I hadn't realized it until I said it, but the same could be said for all of us. Somehow, in just the few weeks that Dimitri had been working with us, all the Pinecones looked a bit sleeker, a little more fit.

We went out into the gym. Heidi was doing her warm-ups. I sat down next to her. "I wasn't really complaining about Dimitri in the locker room. Honest."

Heidi just grunted.

"Don't you believe me?"

She just sighed. "Lauren, look, I've got work to do. I told you all what I think."

I grimaced. Heidi stood up. Darlene lay down beside me and started her stretches.

"What do you really think about Dimitri?" I asked her.

78

"I'm too tired to think," Darlene said. "But I'll tell you, if Heidi thinks one thing and Becky thinks another, I'll go with Heidi every time."

"Yeah, but the other Pinecones are beginning to turn against Dimitri," I said. "They're really buying the line that he's some kind of monster."

Darlene just looked at me. "Who was the one who first called him Dracenstein?" she asked me.

16

Master of Deceit

I always like being at home for a meet. It's a lot easier to do tricks in your own gym. The apparatus all feels familiar. There are spots you look for on the ceiling to keep your bearings when you're in the air.

I had expected Dimitri to give us a big pep talk before the meet, but he didn't.

During our warm-up, he seemed to be everywhere, and his eyes were like hawk's eyes.

Normally when we warm up for a meet we do our routines at only about quarter speed, but with Dimitri watching us it was as if there was no other way to go than full out. Coach Miller was staring at Dimitri with his hands on his hips.

Dimitri ignored him. He was busy on the side-lines, piling up the mats. I thought at first that Dimitri hadn't even seen Coach Miller, but Dimitri leaned down and whispered to me. "Now, vhile he's vatching, ve do the Vickorskoff vault onto the mats. He'll have a fit."

I giggled. Dimitri started to frown at me. Then he grinned. He put his arm on my shoulder and guided me over to the mats.

"I can do it on the horse now," I said.

Dimitri shook his head.

I ran down the runway hard, then I threw my-self into my cartwheel and hit the springboard just right. I landed feet first on the mats.

The Amazons had turned absolutely silent.

I clapped my hands together and ran back to Dimitri. "Did you see me?" I asked excitedly. "I nailed that sucker. I can do it in the meet. We'll wipe the floor with them."

Dimitri was shaking his head. "Not ready yet," he said. "You do the other vault."

"What?" I protested. "Dimitri, I did it better than I ever have in practice."

Dimitri just kept shaking his head. "Too soon. Now we've got them scared."

"But . . . but, that's crazy," I argued.

Dimitri looked down at me. His eyes looked angry. "Shh, you can't let them see that you would argue with me. Go!" Dimitri pointed to the tumbling mats. I still had my floor exercise to warm up on. Patrick was spotting the other Pinecones on their floor exercises.

I walked over and watched Cindi finish. She looked crisper than she ever had before.

"What are you scowling about?" asked Jodi.

"Dimitri," I said.

"Now what did he do?" Jodi asked.

"He won't let me do my new vault," I said. "And I nailed it just a minute ago on the mats. I'm hot, and all he can say is 'not rrready.' "

Jodi glanced over at me. "I thought you said he was pushing you too hard," she said.

I pushed my lips together. Patrick was motioning me to get ready to do my floor exercise. I was so furious that I almost had too much energy doing my tumbling run. I went too far on a couple of my somies. Patrick was shaking his head in amazement.

"Lauren, bottle that energy and use it during the meet," he said.

I walked out into the middle of the mats. Patrick was still my main coach. He'd want me to win, and I knew I could win with my new vault.

"What's wrong?" Patrick asked me.

"You've always been able to read my mind," I said.

"It's not hard," said Patrick. "One of the things I like about you is that you can't hide what you're feeling. What's up? We've only got a few minutes before the meet."

"It's Dimitri!" I said. "He's just nuts. First he works me to the bone learning that Vickorskoff vault, and now he won't let me try it. I want to do it for this meet. We can blow the Amazons away."

Patrick shook his head. "If Dimitri says you're not ready, you're not."

"What? *You're* the boss."

"This has nothing to do with who's the boss. When you get that vault good enough for Dimitri, it'll be good enough for any judge anywhere," said Patrick. "If he says you're not ready, you're not ready."

"But I just did it!"

"You did it in practice," said Patrick.

"But Patrick," I begged, "you're my *real* coach. You know me better than anybody."

Patrick just sighed. "Lauren, right before a meet is no time to discuss this. There's no one whose opinion I respect more than Dimitri's. He's a fireball, and yet he doesn't want to see any of you hurt. It's a dynamite combination. Now listen to him."

I sighed. I knew there was no arguing with Patrick. I went back to the bench.

"What were you talking about with Patrick?" Becky asked me. "Were you telling him that Dimitri is pushing you Pinecones too hard?"

I felt very confused. "No, Becky, that's not the problem. Patrick and Dimitri won't let me try my new vault, and I know I can do it."

"Maybe Dimitri's secretly working for Coach Miller," Becky whispered. "You know we first saw him here. Maybe this has all been one of Coach Miller's tricks." She winked at me.

"Becky," I sighed, "I can't even begin to think about that right before the meet."

"Well, maybe you don't want to think about it," said Becky, "but I think you should. You and I are the only ones to see through him."

"Becky," I said, "Patrick just finished telling me for the umpteenth time that Dimitri's a master and we all have to learn from him."

"Master of deceit," whispered Becky. "And only you and I know it."

There it was again. Becky and I, what a combination. But what if Becky was right? I watched as Dimitri went up to Coach Miller and shook his hand.

What *if* this whole thing was just a Dimitri plot, and I was one of his pawns?

Scraping the Bottom of the Barrel

Despite my worries, everything seemed to be going the Pinecones' way. Cindi pulled off the most spectacular bar routine of her life, and she ended up winning on bars. But two Amazons came in second and third. Darlene won on beam, and Ti An came in second. Jodi, to everyone's surprise, came in second on the floor exercise. I tied for second in vault. The Amazons got first and second.

Because we had split so many events it was hard to tell which team was ahead on points.

Dimitri was pacing up and down in back of the judges. At least the judge who had given me the deduction wasn't there.

"He looks like a caged bear," said Jodi.

"Yeah, but I wonder which side he's really on," I said. I bit the nail of my thumb, something I always do when I'm nervous.

Finally the judges stood up. The head judge took the microphone. "This was an exceedingly close match," he said. "The winning team, however, is the Atomic Amazons."

I was watching Dimitri closely. He made a fist with his right hand and pounded it into his left. His eyes were blazing.

He came over to us. "You girls did goo-ooood," he said. "You hold your heads up. They are scared. For two veeks they vill think of nothing but how close you came. It's goo-ood."

Jodi giggled. "You know, that guy grows on you."

I just bit my thumb. "Wait till I talk to you in the locker room," I whispered.

The locker room was full of jubilation as if we had won, not lost. Darlene and Cindi held their trophies high in the air, and were slapping each other's palms. Jodi stood on one of the benches and took a bucket of ice and poured it over Darlene's head.

"We're almost number one! We're almost number one!" chanted Jodi. The rest of the Pinecones chimed in.

Normally I would have been in the thick of it. Instead I felt like a wet blanket.

Darlene noticed me, sitting on the bench. "Hey, Lauren!" she yelled, wiping the ice water off her face. "Why so glum? You tied for second. You were great."

"Yeah, but what if I could have gotten a first?" I said.

"Next time," said Cindi cheerfully. "Next time you'll do it. With Dimitri coaching us, we're going to be invincible."

"Yeah," said Jodi. "It might mean a lifetime of two-a-day Saturday practices, but look at the results. You know, winning is fun."

"We didn't win today," I argued.

"Yeah, but we sure came close," said Jodi. "You've got to give Dimitri credit. We've never been so good. All of us."

I shook my head. "What if it's Dimitri who *wants* us to lose?"

The rest of the Pinecones stopped their celebrating and stared at me.

"What's that supposed to mean?" Jodi asked.

"It's just something that Becky said to me," I admitted. "I tell you, I was ready to do the new vault, and the only one who stopped me was Dimitri."

"Becky said *what?*" asked Darlene. Her voice was low.

"Becky just reminded me we first saw Dimitri at the Atomic Amazons," I said. "Dimitri is known to be the master of deceit. What if Coach Miller paid him to come here and try to sabotage us?"

Darlene came over to me and put her hand on my forehead. "You've got Dimitri brain fever," she said.

I giggled nervously.

Darlene didn't laugh back. "It's not so funny, Lauren," she said. "Ever since Dimitri's come here, you've been running around like a chicken with its head cut off. It's time to fish or cut bait."

"Chicken, fish," I teased. "You make me sound like a restaurant menu." All the Pinecones knew that I loved food.

Nobody laughed.

"It's not funny anymore," said Cindi. "Who are you going to trust? Becky, or Dimitri and us?"

"Dimitri *and* us?" I demanded. "Since when did it become Dimitri *and* us? A while ago, on our first Saturday workout, you were agreeing with me that he was Dracenstein."

"That was a joke," said Cindi. "But you can't argue with success. It's not just the trophies. We *are* different. It shows."

"And it doesn't mean that we're still not loyal to Patrick," said Darlene. "Patrick's not asking us to choose between him and Dimitri. Why do you make it an either-or?"

I looked up at her.

88

"But what about what Becky said?" I protested. My arguments sounded weak, even to me.

"Becky?" pooh-poohed Cindi. "Come on, Lauren, when you have to quote Becky, you're scraping the bottom of the barrel."

Cindi was right.

18

Being a Bug Isn't So Bad

It was our last Saturday workout before our next meet with the Amazons.

I wasn't as tired as when we had first started doing the twice-a-day workouts. My body had gotten stronger.

Dimitri was working with Heidi on her vault. I watched as she seemed to fly toward the ceiling, adding an extra twist that I had never seen before.

Becky and I watched her. "She's going to kill herself," Becky muttered.

"No, she won't," I said.

"Well, he's killing me," said Becky. "I told Patrick I've had it."

"What did Patrick say?" I asked her.

"He said it was my decision," said Becky. "But my mind's made up. I'm not going to work with that mad Hungarian. And if you're smart, you won't do it, either."

Heidi did her new vault again. This time she went even higher. Dimitri ran up to her after she had landed and gave her a bear hug. Heidi doesn't show her emotions easily, but she hugged him back.

"Pretty soon the world vill be calling it 'the Ferguson twist,' " said Dimitri, patting Heidi on the shoulder. "Ve show them something new, surprise them."

Heidi grinned back at him. She went to the bench and toweled off.

"That was fantastic," I said to her.

Heidi nodded. She knew she was good. "Dimitri and I made that up," she said.

"Okay, Lauren. Your turn," said Dimitri. He didn't even look at Becky. Patrick must have told him that Becky didn't want to work with him anymore.

I chalked up. "Remember, think head in line vith the trunk," said Dimitri. "That vay you von't get hurt."

I closed my eyes. Head in line with the trunk, toes pointed, hands flexed. If I tried to remember everything that Dimitri had drilled into me day after day, I'd go crazy.

I ran and hit the springboard, and dived backward for the horse. My hands hit the leather, and I bounced up. I landed squarely on my feet.

I looked at Dimitri, waiting for him to tell me what I had done wrong. "I can point my feet more," I said before he could open his mouth.

Dimitri laughed. "Goo-ood," he said. "Von more time."

"You really mean twenty-six more times, don't you?" I said.

Dimitri put his arm around me. "Yes," he said. "I knew from the first day I saw you that you vere a fighter. And I pushed you. I know that. I knew you vere sore, and somedays you think, 'Who is this man? He's crazy,' but that's vhy I say 'von more time,' to see if you'll do it. You're a bug."

"Why do you keep calling me a bug?" I asked. "It's not a very nice thing to call somebody."

"A bug jumps. It lives. It's not afraid. Vhat should I call you?" he asked.

I looked at him. Suddenly being called a bug didn't seem so bad.

I got ready to do the vault "von more time."

19

Strong! Bang! High! Blam!

We walked into the Atomic Amazons gym, and I saw her right away, even before we had begun our warm-ups. I put my gym bag on the floor and wailed, "Oh, no! She's back."

"Now what?" asked Darlene.

"Look," I said. I didn't want to point, so I nudged with my chin toward the judges' bench. "That's the one. The one who's got it in for me," I muttered. "I might as well pack it in right now."

The judge was chatting with Coach Miller and smiling up at him. "I'm sunk," I said.

"That's not exactly the winning attitude we're supposed to be knocking 'em dead with," said Jodi.

"I know," I admitted. "But why did she have to show up today of all days?"

Dimitri and Patrick came up to us. "Vhat's wrong?" Dimitri growled. "Vhy do you stop here like a bunch of dead ducks?"

"Because that's what we're going to be," I said. "Look, Patrick. It's the same judge. It's got to be some conspiracy that she's here again."

"Lauren," said Patrick, "there aren't that many USGF certified judges *in* Denver. You were bound to run into her again."

My shoulders slumped. "Just my luck it had to be today," I sighed.

Suddenly I felt a strong hand on my shoulder, turning me around. "Ve turn it around," said Dimitri.

I nodded. "Right, you just turned me around." I thought it was another of Dimitri's language problems. I didn't understand what it had to do with the judge.

"No, no," growled Dimitri. "It vill be good luck. Look at me. Vhat is my name?"

I tried to look for Patrick. Maybe Dimitri was having some kind of flashback to Hungary and had forgotten who he was.

"Uh, Dimitri Vickorskoff," I said, nervously.

Dimitri nodded as if I had just won *Jeopardy*. "And what vault do you do today, for the first time in competition?" Dimitri asked me.

"The Vickorskoff," I answered.

Dimitri nodded again. He thumped his breast. "I invented the vault. The judge vill know I'm there, vatching her. She *knows* I never let a gymnast try something in competition unless I think she'll be perfect. All the time the judge is marking, she vill be thinking of me."

Dimitri pointed a finger at me. "You, you have nothing to vorry about. Go varm up. And no long faces. All of you. You are roosters. Nasty roosters."

"Dimitri's right, Lauren," said Patrick. "That judge will have a full plate, just watching out for Dimitri. There are a lot of advantages having him on our side. Now go stretch out. We'll meet you for the warm-ups."

I watched as Dimitri walked toward the judge, a big smile on his face. The smile on Coach Miller's face faded fast.

"I think we're going to have a *good* time today," said Jodi.

We swung into our warm-ups. We were much more intense than we had ever been before. While the Amazons did five or six stretches, we did fifteen. They did parts of their routines for their warm-ups. We nailed one complete routine after another. And all the time, the judges were watching us.

Everything went just right for us in practice.

Vaults were sticking, bars were swinging. We all felt positive, and after each warm-up, Dimitri and Patrick were there, pumping us up.

At the judge's announcement of the official start of the meet, we marched in. I could hear my parents shouting for us.

I knew the vault was first. I was going to go last for our team.

I watched the Atomic Amazons do the Yamashita. It looked so simple to me now. To think that just a little over a month ago, I had thought that I would never do a harder vault.

The Amazons did nothing dynamic, but they landed everything solid. The last of the Atomic Amazons did her vault almost perfectly. She got a 9.9, a higher score than I thought she deserved.

I bit my lip.

Heidi knew what was happening right away. "They're making it hard for you," she whispered to me, as we watched Darlene, Cindi, Jodi, and Ashley do their vaults. They all scored high, 9.6's and 9.7's. We were certainly giving the Amazons a run for their money, but they were still ahead.

Ti An was the one before me. She had mastered the Yamashita, and she landed it great. The only mistake I could see was a little break in her hands as she hit the horse.

Dimitri stood beside me as we waited for Ti An's score. They gave her only a 9.6.

"Ti An's vault was better than that," I said, turning to Dimitri. I was furious. It was so unfair.

I saw the anger in Dimitri's eyes. "It's all right," he said angrily. "It's a fight, and ve vill fight them."

I nodded and bit my lip. I didn't know how I was supposed to fight a judge who was unfair to our team.

"Hey," said Dimitri, "I tell you, it's going to be all right."

Patrick came up to us. "Are you ready?" he asked me.

I tried to swallow. "Don't hold back," said Patrick. "Go for it. You have nothing to lose."

Dimitri was nodding his head for emphasis with every word that Patrick said.

"Listen to me," said Dimitri. "Run strong, then bang! Hit it! Then high. Strong, bang, high, blam! Okay?"

It might not be perfect English, but I knew exactly what Dimitri meant.

Patrick and Dimitri moved away from the runway. Now it was up to me. I could see Dimitri pacing up and down in back of the judges' table.

I thought of all the practice vaults Dimitri had forced on me. I knew this move inside and out.

I raised my hand and saluted the judge. I took my position. I could feel my adrenalin pumping.

I hurdled into my roundoff; I hit the springboard with my hands, and I was off in space. I had plenty of time to reach back with my hands, and the horse was right where it had always been. I pushed off, high, high, and then I bent my knees as I landed, fighting to keep my balance. Both my hands went up. I had stuck it so hard I swear I could feel the floor shake.

I heard a whoop and a holler from my teammates. I ran off.

Dimitri swept me into his arms in a bear hug. "That's it! That's it! Fantastic!"

I looked up. I hadn't even known that "fantastic" was in Dimitri's vocabulary.

"No 'one more time'?" I teased him. Dimitri wasn't listening. He was looking over at the judges' table. They were conferring. Patrick came up to us. He gave me a hug, too. "That was beautiful," he said, "just beautiful."

"What's going on with the judges?" I asked nervously.

The other Pinecones surrounded me, patting me on the back, but still the judges didn't come up with their score.

"They must be having an argument," said Patrick.

Finally the score went up. 9.95. I couldn't believe it. Not only had I won the trophy for the vault, but I had pulled the Pinecones ahead.

I raised my hands over my head like a boxer and grinned at my parents.

"Enough," said Dimitri.

I lowered my arms quickly. "You're right. I shouldn't gloat," I whispered.

Dimitri patted me on the shoulder. "No, no, it's okay," he said. "But next time, ve try for a ten."

About the Author

Elizabeth Levy decided that the only way she could write about gymnastics was to try it herself. Besides taking classes, she is involved with a group of young gymnasts near her home in New York City and enjoys following their progress.

Elizabeth Levy's other Apple Paperbacks are *A Different Twist*, *The Computer That Said Steal Me*, and all the other books in THE GYMNASTS series.

She likes visiting schools to give talks and meet her readers. Kids love her presentations. Why? "I start with a cartwheel!" says Levy. "At least I try to."

APPLE PAPERBACKS

THE GYMNASTS™

by Elizabeth Levy

Available wherever you buy books, or use this order form.

Scholastic Inc., P.O. Box 7502, 2931 East McCarty Street, Jefferson City, MO 65102

Please send me the books I have checked above. I am enclosing $_____ (please add $2.00 to cover shipping and handling). Send check or money order — no cash or C.O.D.s please.

Name _____

Address _____

City _____ State/Zip _____

by Ann M. Martin

The seven girls at Stoneybrook Middle School get into all kinds
of adventures...with school, boys, and, of course, baby-sitting!

SLEEPOVER FRIENDS™
by Susan Saunders

Available wherever you buy books...or use this order form.

Scholastic Inc. P.O. Box 7502, 2931 E. McCarty Street, Jefferson City, MO 65102

Please send me the books I have checked above. I am enclosing $ _____

(please add $2.00 to cover shipping and handling). Send check or money order—no cash or C.O.D.s please.

Name _____

Address _____

City_____ State/Zip _____

Please allow four to six weeks for delivery. Offer good in U.S.A. only. Sorry, mail orders are not available to residents of Canada. Prices subject to change.

SF1190